SMUDGED

Tales Across Time

NANDITA CHAKRAVERTI

Chennai • Bangalore

CLEVER FOX PUBLISHING
Chennai, India

Published by CLEVER FOX PUBLISHING 2025

ISBN: 978-93-7500-374-8

ABOUT THE AUTHOR

Nandita Chakraverti is a Mumbai-based writer, storyteller, and spirited senior citizen who brings heart, history, and imagination to everything she does. Over the past 25 years, she has built her family's investment and trading business from scratch — a journey marked by solitude, resilience and grace. An advocate for women's financial empowerment, Nandita believes that confidence and dignity begin with understanding one's own worth — emotionally and economically.

Her creative journey began with poetry at the age of ten, and has since blossomed into rich storytelling inspired by her deep love for nature, travel, and the wild heart of India. Whether tracing the silent paths of tigers and leopards in the forests of Bandhavgarh, Pench, Kanaha Tadoba, Corbett or observing the snow-capped stillness of the Himalayas, Nandita writes with the keen eye of a traveller and the tender heart of a dreamer.

Her debut children's book, Coco: A Cat's Magical Journey, invites young readers into a whimsical world of friendship, courage, and adventure — guided by a talking cat, a wise grasshopper, an adorable ant, and a mischievous raccoon.

When she's not writing stories or exploring far-flung corners of the world, Nandita shares reflections on tiger sightings, unusual destinations, and senior citizen rights through thoughtful articles and engaging Social media posts. To her, every stage of life is a chance to grow — and every story is a gift to be shared.

Author's Note - Smudged: Tales across Time

Sometimes, the past doesn't stay buried. It lingers — in old houses, forgotten photographs, a whiff of jasmine on a winter night. Smudged: Tales Across Time grew from such moments. A flicker of intuition. A childhood memory that never quite made sense. The quiet feeling that someone was watching — not with malice, but with memory.

These stories span decades of my life and imagination, many drawn from real places — the tigers and leopards of Sal forests of India, the solemn corridors of Hijli Jail, the windswept deserts of Rajasthan, and even the warm bustle of city streets where a beagle like Sushi might just save the day. I've met many kinds of ghosts in my time — the kind that float, and the kind that stay behind in our hearts.

I believe stories are never just fiction. They're emotions in disguise. A way of remembering what history forgets. A way of making sense of what logic cannot explain. Through these pages, I invite you to listen — not just with your ears, but with the soft corners of your heart.

> *You may or may not you believe in ghosts, I do believe... they believe in you.*
>
> **– Nandita**

CONTENTS

INTRODUCTION

Smudged: Tales Across Time is a collection that walks the fine line between memory and myth, reality and reverie.

These are not just ghost stories. They are stories of people — and the invisible threads that bind them to places, moments, and other lives

I've always believed that stories don't begin on paper — they begin as feelings. A scent that lingers too long. A place that refuses to be forgotten. A voice you're sure you've heard before but can't quite place. Smudged: Tales Across Time was born out of such moments — elusive, insistent, and deeply human.

These stories were written across decades, many inspired by real places, real events, and sometimes... real silences. My travels to the tiger reserves of India, lonely nights in historic colonial towns, the forgotten corridors of Hijli Jail — each carried a pulse, a presence. Not always frightening. Often gentle. Always unforgettable.

Ghosts, for me, are not just figures in white sheets or creaking floorboards. They are memories that never left. Feelings we never quite resolved. They might take the shape of a beagle named Sushi, a sceptic lost in the desert, or a child peering through a crack in time. They may even live in libraries or in the shadows of trees you pass every day. Whether you believe in them or not doesn't matter. What matters is: do you listen?

This book is not only about hauntings. It's about grief, wonder, injustice, and love — and the extraordinary ways the past insists on being remembered. Some tales come from whispered family stories. Others from headlines that never left me. A few are pure imagination — but then again, aren't all memories a little smudged?

To those who've ever felt watched by something kind.

To those who've ever heard a lullaby in a rustling tree.

To those who've lost... and still feel the presence of what was once found —

These stories are for you.

Some stories are embroidered with imagination. Others emerge like breath on cold glass — lingering, half-visible, waiting for someone to notice..

Set against rich, evocative backdrops — from the desolate sands of Rajasthan to the mist-laced stairwells of haunted colleges, from the echoing cells of Hijli Jail to the whimsical lanes of old Mumbai — each tale peers into a realm just beyond reach. Sometimes tragic, sometimes tender, these are stories where the land speaks, and time folds upon itself. Places hold memory. Objects hum with longing. Animals know things we don't. And people — living or otherwise — search for connection, closure, or simply a voice to hear them.

You will meet:

A lone man and a silent passenger in The Backseat.

50-year-old crosses lifetimes in The Tale of Teen Sukhia.

A beagle named Sushi, whose instincts guard not just space, but soul.

A question whispered to the universe — Why Me? — and the unsettling reply it receives.

The invisible roar of ancestral felines in Tiger Calling.

A hardened engineer brought to his knees by sand, silence, and those who are Guardians

The knowledge of the dead stored among the shelves of The Whispering Library in the House of St Barnabas.

And in Hijli Jail: Hauntings, the unfinished dreams of revolutionaries that still echo in stone and shadow.

Some tales are inspired by real incidents flashes of truth beneath fiction's veil. Others grow from feelings you cannot shake off: déjà vu, a breath on your neck, a song you've never heard but somehow remember. These are stories where ghosts don't rattle chains; they nudge memories. They don't always seek revenge — just remembrance.

In India, where myth often overlaps with morning chai, and memory is layered like old saris in a steel trunk, belief is not always required. But attention is. These stories ask for it. Because ghosts — real or imagined — do not demand belief. Only that you listen.

So, step in. Light a lamp. Open the door just a crack.

And let the stories speak.

As a child, I often sensed things before I saw them — a soft presence, a shadow on the edge of light, a memory that didn't seem like mine. Perhaps it was imagination. Or perhaps the world is kinder and more mysterious than we allow ourselves to believe. These stories are my way of listening in — of letting forgotten voices speak.

The pages you hold are woven from many threads: the solemn silence of Hijli Jail, where revolution once stirred behind iron bars… the golden dust of Rajasthan where ancient winds carry forgotten names… the dark canopy of tiger forests where time itself seems to pause… and sometimes, the narrow lanes of a modern city where a dog named Sushi sniffs out truths long hidden.

Each tale in Smudged has its own pulse — some soft and wistful, others sharp and unsettling. But all of them, I believe, are about the unseen bonds between worlds. They are not horror stories. They are human stories — with a shadowed edge. The kind that sit quietly in your heart long after you've read the last line.

I have long believed that stories are not just fiction. They are emotion in disguise. They are how we remember what history forgets, how we mourn without words, how we pass on what must not be lost. The ghosts in these tales are not always meant to frighten. Some come bearing comfort. Some remind us of mistakes. And some… simply want to be known.

If you've ever looked over your shoulder at dusk, or felt the weight of an old memory in a familiar place, I hope these stories will feel like home.

With love,

Nandita

THE BACKSEAT

It was nearing 9 p.m. when I left the mechanic's garage on my old two-wheeler. The winter wind had a bite, and the town had already begun to close in on itself for the night. I zipped up my jacket and took the back road home—faster, quieter, and winding through the outer edge of town. That road always felt a little off. Too still, too silent. Tonight, it was worse.

A sliver of moon hung low as I passed the rusted gate of the old Hindu cremation ground. The land beyond was thick with trees, the mounds barely visible in the gloom. I kept my eyes on the road, but something shifted beneath me.

The scooter dipped slightly—as if someone had just climbed on behind me.

My hands tightened on the handlebar.

I didn't stop. I didn't look back. Maybe the road was uneven. Maybe I was tired.

A minute later, the scooter began to struggle—subtly, but enough to notice. The engine groaned more than usual. It felt like riding uphill, though the road was flat.

And then I felt it.

Pressure.

It was a weight on the seat behind me.

A weight that hadn't been there before.

I told myself not to look. I stared straight ahead, my heartbeat tapping against my ribcage like a second engine.

The chill around me deepened—not the kind that came from wind, but something slower, crawling into the space between skin and bone. That's when I heard it. A faint sound, barely audible above the engine's buzz. Breathing. Shallow. Measured. Close—too close. I gripped the throttle and sped up, the engine whining. Houses began to appear. Streetlights flickered into view. Suddenly, as I crossed the main junction, the scooter felt lighter, as if a weight had lifted.

I didn't stop until I reached home. I parked, ran inside, and shut the door behind me, hands shaking.

Only when I sat down did I realise—I had never once looked back.

I still use that road occasionally.

However, I never pass the cremation ground without feeling as if I am being watched.

And I never ride with an empty backseat. My back seat has a basket of books or odds and ends in a basket tied to the seat carriage… There is no space for anyone to sit.

The Florist's Boy

A month before, Ravi, the florist's teenage son, had taken the same back road one evening to deliver a garland to the temple priest's home. His father had been very busy, so Ravi volunteered. It was just a few minutes away by cycle.

He swore something strange happened as he passed the cremation ground.

"I was pedalling like normal," he told his mother later, voice shaking. "But the garland inside the cloth bag felt like it got heavier on my handlebar. I thought maybe it snagged on something. I looked down. Nothing."

When he looked up again, the road ahead shimmered slightly—like heat waves rising from asphalt, even though it was a cold night.

"And then I heard it—someone crying…"

Ravi had stopped, confused. There was no one around. Just the rustling trees and an old funeral pyre stump.

He turned around and went back the long way, garland still in hand. When he gave it to the priest, the man took one look at it and froze.

It was wet. Completely soaked through, as if dunked in river water.

But Ravi swore it had never left the dry cloth bag.

The Retired Postmaster

Fifteen years ago, Mr Bose, long retired and known in town for his quiet manner, had once been the postmaster who delivered telegrams to the cremation ground caretaker and the locals.

He didn't speak much of those days. But after hearing whispers of others' experiences, he finally shared his own.

"That road is old. Older than the town," he began. "One winter night I was returning from the station on foot—no scooter back then. I had just crossed the cremation wall when I saw a figure just ahead. I thought she might've been a mourner. But as I walked past… she wasn't there. She never turned. Never moved. And yet—" he hesitated, "I felt something slip past me. Cold. Grief, like a presence. Too heavy for one heart."

When he reached home, he found one of the sealed letters in his satchel had been opened. Not torn. Opened—neatly, deliberately.

It was a condolence telegram. To a family who had lost their daughter. In a fire.

Mr Bose never used that road again.

Back to the Narrator

I heard these stories much later—over tea, in whispers, from neighbours who once brushed off my own.

But the town remembers, quietly.

And me? I still take that road.

I still don't look back.

And I still ride with the seat full.

Even when I'm alone.

Just in case…

The Vanishing Rider.

Suresh locked up Patel & Sons General Store well past midnight, the metallic clatter of the shutters breaking the silence of the deserted street. His family had run this shop for three generations. Its wooden counters bore the worn polish of decades, and its walls still hung with fading calendars from years gone by.

He kicked his scooter to life and took the old road home—the one skirting the crematorium. It was faster, yes, but also notorious. People spoke of odd shapes under the banyan tree and voices that seemed to ride the wind. Suresh always dismissed it. Tonight, though, the road felt emptier than usual.

A mile in, he felt it: the shift. His scooter dipped ever so slightly, as if an unseen weight pressed down on the pillion seat. His fingers locked on the handles. His grandfather's words came back unbidden:

"If you feel it, boy… never turn around."

The hum of his engine filled the night. He drove faster, eyes glued to the beam of light ahead.

Then he saw it. Near the old banyan tree, just by the crematorium gate—a figure. Tall and thin, draped in something that seemed more shadow than cloth.

A chill ran through him.

It looked—no, it reminded him—of his grandaunt Kamala, the spinster whose sepia-toned portrait hung in the anteroom of his house, among the other departed ancestors. She had been strange in life, whispered about in hushed tones, a woman who died alone in her narrow room, childless and half-forgotten.

He dared a glance in the rearview mirror. For a split second, he thought he saw her face reflected there: hollow-eyed, lips curling faintly, not in kindness but recognition.

By the time he skidded into his courtyard, his shirt clung to him like a second skin. He parked, trembling, and forced himself to look back.

The seat was wet, but it hadn't rained in days.

Someone had been sitting there moments before. A faint smell of old camphor and ashes hung in the air.

Inside the anteroom, he passed by the portraits of his ancestors.

His eyes stopped at Kamala's. It eerily matched the figure under the banyan tree.

He stared at it for a long time before daring to turn away.

The Taxi Driver's Fare

Rafiq, a taxi driver, once picked up a man near the edge of town. The stranger asked to be dropped "near the old cremation ground". Quiet ride, no small talk.

When they reached the spot, Rafiq turned to ask for payment. The back seat was empty.

The door hadn't opened. He sped away, but the faint smell of sandalwood smoke lingered in the car for days—the kind used in last rites.

The narrator talks of the tourist journalist who had come to chronicle the ghost story of the backseat passenger.

Here's a chilling yet atmospheric story of the tourist journalist who came to investigate the legend of The Backseat Passenger:

The TRAVEL BLOGGER Sabbir…

A travel journalist known for chasing local legends arrived in town one winter evening. He had heard whispers of an old road haunted by "the backseat passenger"—a figure tied to the ruins of an ancient crematorium built centuries before the town itself.

Determined to uncover the truth, he rented a scooter and set out late at night, the recorder on, narrating every detail.

"The road is silent," he spoke into the mic. "No headlights behind me, no houses in sight. The old cremation ground lies just ahead. Locals say that those who pass here at night never ride alone. As his scooter approached the rusted gates, he felt it—an unmistakable dip in the seat. A sudden weight on the seat. He gripped the handlebars tighter, breath fogging the cold night air. "The scooter feels… heavier," his voice trembled into the recorder.

The engine strained as though dragging someone uphill, even on flat ground. The air smelt faintly of smoke—ancient sandalwood, burnt long ago.

And then came the whisper. A single word: "Stop." Another word "home".

He could hear his heart pounding as he braked near the old banyan tree by the crematorium. The scooter's engine died. Slowly, almost mechanically, he turned his head.

Empty.

But his recorder had captured it: a second voice, soft and hollow, saying, 'Stop," "Home."

He fled, leaving the scooter behind, sprinting until the lights of the town came into view.

The next morning, locals found the scooter parked neatly outside the cremation ground gate. No keys. No footprints.

The travel blogger did publish this story. A few scoffed at his write-up. A FAIR NUMBER were RATHER EXCITED. Within three years, the excitement had died down.

But the recorder—

It still plays that whisper.

The Journalist's Ride

Ananya Roy, a travel journalist famed for her bold ghost chronicles, arrived in the small town to investigate whispers of

"The Backseat Passenger"—a figure tied to an ancient cremation ground older than the road itself.

Locals warned her, "That land was sacred once. No one goes near it after dark." But warnings were invitations to her.

One moonless night, recorder in hand, she rode a rented scooter down the desolate stretch.

"This is the old road," her voice quivered into the mic. "It cuts past the ruins of the crematorium. They say it predates the town by two centuries. No priests tend it now. The pyres burnt out long ago… but they say one spirit never left."

As she neared the rusted gates, the scooter dipped sharply. The air thickened. The faint scent of sandalwood smoke—old, dry—wrapped around her. "The seat feels… heavier," she whispered.

And then it came: a voice, close as breath. One word.

"Stop."

Heart hammering, she braked near the ancient banyan tree. The engine sputtered and died. The whisper returned:

"Home."

Shaking, Ananya turned.

No one was there. The next morning, she dug through old town records at the municipal office. What she found chilled her:

In 1817, a plague swept through the village. A young woman—never named—was cremated hurriedly, without rites, on that very ground. Locals believed her spirit lingered, waiting for the final prayers that never came.

Some said the road was cursed because it cut across her resting place. Others say her ghost rode along with travellers seeking passage home.

Ananya's recorder captured it all: her narration, her breathing… at the end, a faint, mournful voice:

"Light the fire.

That night, a group of locals went to the cremation ground with offerings—marigolds, incense, and flame. They whispered mantras, hands trembling. Since then, sightings dwindled. But those who still take that road after dark say the scooter seat sometimes dips—just slightly—as though someone grateful has finally found peace.

And Ananya's article?

It ends with one chilling line:

"I rode alone that night. But I never felt alone."

The Parapsychologist's Visit

A British parapsychologist had heard about this story from a couple who visited this town in India 15 years ago; therefore, he came to examine it using a parapsychologist's perspective.

Dr Edward Halloway was not a man easily swayed by ghost stories. An Oxford-trained parapsychologist, his fieldwork had taken him from abandoned asylums in Yorkshire to the misty battlefields of Normandy. But it was an English couple he'd once interviewed—tourists who spoke of a chilling encounter on a deserted road in eastern India—that drew him across continents.

"A scooter ride past an old cremation ground," the woman had said, visibly shaken even after 15 years. "A weight behind us… breathing that wasn't ours."

Halloway arrived in the town during the monsoon lull, determined to separate folklore from phenomenon.

Day 1: The Ground

He began at the ruins of the ancient crematorium—a site older than the town itself, overgrown with banyan roots and silence. He carried his EMF meter, digital voice recorder, and thermal camera.

Locals told him of a plague in 1817, of hurried cremations without rites. A municipal clerk produced faded records: dozens of unnamed dead, one location repeatedly mentioned—"north pyre".

As dusk fell, he recorded spikes in electromagnetic readings near that very site. The air felt denser, not humid but charged, like before a lightning strike. His equipment noted a 6°C temperature drop over ten minutes, confined to a circular area roughly three meters wide. "Localised anomaly," he muttered, taking notes.

Day 2: The Road

That night, Halloway rode a rented scooter down the same stretch described in the accounts. His camera fixed behind him, his recorder pinned near his collar.

At precisely 11:47 p.m., near the cremation ground gates, he documented:

Seat displacement: The scooter dipped, verified by suspension compression sensors.

Audio evidence: A faint exhalation, human-like, on the recorder.

Olfactory anomaly: The scent of sandalwood—detectable despite wind direction and absence of sources.

He felt it too: a distinct weight on the backseat, paired with a sudden pressure drop in his ears.

"If psychosomatic, it's remarkably consistent with prior reports," he dictated, though his pulse betrayed unease.

Day 3: The Whisper

Reviewing the audio, Halloway found it: at 11:48 p.m., beneath the engine hum, a whisper. Single word.

"Home."

He played it twenty times, spectral analysis confirming it was not engine noise, not wind, and not his own voice. Formant frequencies matched a female vocal range.

Conclusion

In his report, Halloway stopped short of calling it proof of haunting. Instead, he framed it in measured terms:

"The phenomena observed—auditory, tactile, electromagnetic—suggest a persistent imprint tied to this site. Whether residual or interactive remains undetermined. The historical record of disrupted funerary rites correlates strikingly with local oral tradition. Further controlled investigation is warranted."

But in private notes—never published—he added one line:

"When I crossed the junction and the weight lifted, I glanced back at the empty seat. It was empty… but it didn't feel empty."
Some rides stay with you.

Even if your backseat stays empty.

KACHORIS
POHA

THE TALE OF TEEN SUKHIA

Every morning before the world stirred, Teen Sukhia was awake by 4 a.m., stoking the coals and steaming pots of chai, poha, and kachoris on his handcart. By 9:30, the food was gone, his regulars were fed, and the cart was wiped clean. Then he returned to his other life—pulling his rickshaw through the shaded lanes of Dehradun, ferrying children to school, housewives to the Haat, and stooped grandmothers who had known him since he was a wiry boy of ten.

Everyone knew him by his pet name—Teen Sukhia, the third-born after two sisters, his arrival once celebrated as happiness. Now, in his fifties, he looked decades older. His face was a map of wrinkles, cheerful but weary, his legs knotted with muscle and varicose veins that gave him the gait of an ex-footballer. At home, nine hungry mouths waited, along with a dying grandmother and memories of a father swallowed in the Uttarakhand floods forty years ago. The remittances never stopped, even if his visits home came only once in two years.

That winter night in Dehradun, exhaustion had pulled Teen Sukhia into an early slumber. When he startled awake, he thought it was 4 a.m., time for his usual routine—but the old alarm clock's hands had betrayed him; it was barely 2.

Still, habit ruled him. He boiled the potatoes for kachoris, kneaded the flour, fried the nuts, and chopped chillies and onions. The coal fire glowed red, sending up a fragrant plume. The smell of hot poha and crisping bread drifted into the misty lanes far beyond his ramshackle brick home.

It was then he felt it—the air shift, the cold creep. He turned, and from the doorway three tall shadows emerged. Men in dhotis, heavy shoes, turbans wrapped tight, faces hidden behind thick woollen blankets. Without a word, one gestured toward the food.

His instinct was obedience. He laid out a mat, set down the low wooden chaukis, and placed before them steaming plates of poha and kachoris, pouring scalding tea into tin tumblers. They ate in silence, every bite deliberate, every sip swift.

When finished, one pulled out a wad of notes and placed it on the mat. In a gravelly voice he said, "We will return at the same time tomorrow. Ask no questions." The three rose as one, and with a rustle of cloth, vanished into the fog outside.

Teen Sukhia cleared the plates, his hands trembling. When he finally picked up the wad of cash, his eyes widened—it was the same sum he scrimped and toiled for an entire month, now earned in less than a quarter hour.

The old alarm clock ticked on the shelf. Rubbing his eyes, he looked again—it was barely 3 a.m. He had been awake for his nocturnal visitors, who left before the world even stirred.

And from that night, no matter how he tried, he could never tell whether they were men of flesh and blood… or spirits summoned by the scent of his food.

The Silent Routine

From that night on, the three men returned every single night at 2 a.m.

Their arrival was always the same—the shuffle of shoes on the wet earth, the whisper of thick blankets, turbans gleaming faintly under the moonlight. They stepped into Teen Sukhia's brick home without a word, sat cross-legged on the mat, and ate in silence.

Every night, he prepared the same spread: steaming poha, kachoris, and boiling tea in battered tumblers. Every night, they ate with unhurried precision, leaving behind the same wad of notes on the mat. And every night, before the clock struck 3, they vanished into the fog-choked lanes of Dehradun, swallowed by the eerie mist.

The Winter Grows Colder

The town slept, unaware. The coal fire crackled, shadows flickered against the walls, and Teen Sukhia felt a chill he could never shake. He never dared ask them who they were. Their silence was heavier than words; their eyes—barely visible beneath their turbans—seemed not to belong to the living.

By the second week, he stopped questioning his fortune. His remittances went home heavier than ever, his debts eased, and his children ate well. Yet when he looked at the thick bundles of notes, they seemed damp with mist, as though they carried the smell of river water and long-buried earth.

The Month of Visits

For a full thirty nights, the ritual never broke. The men came, ate, left money, and disappeared. Outside, the streets of Dehradun lay quiet under the fog, only the faint creak of their retreating steps breaking the silence.

Each morning, Teen Sukhia woke from a shallow, unsettled sleep, wondering if it had all been a dream. But the empty plates, the ashes of the coal fire, and the weight of money on his shelf said otherwise.

By the end of the month, he had begun to fear dawn—not for what he might see, but for what he might not. Because part of him knew, with a creeping certainty, that one night they would stop coming. And when they did, the silence they left behind would be more terrifying than their visits ever were.

Five Months of Plenty

For nearly five full months, the three silent visitors kept their pact. Each night, as the mist rolled down Dehradun's lanes, they arrived at 2 a.m., ate in silence, left their money, and vanished before the clock struck 3.

Teen Sukhia's life transformed. His family back home bought two cows for milk and another parcel of land, and their children went to school in clean uniforms. In the village, where poverty had once marked them, they now carried a new respect. Whispers grew that fortune had finally smiled on Teen Sukhia—the man who once looked seventy at fifty now walked with a strange vigour in his step, his wrinkles lit with cheer.

The Night of Kheer

That evening, thrilled by how life had turned, he decided to do something different. Instead of only kachoris and poha, he made kheer, the sweet rice pudding simmered in fresh milk, garnished with nuts and cardamom. The aroma filled his small kitchen, richer than anything he had cooked in years.

When the three men arrived, wrapped in their dhotis and heavy blankets, as always, he served them as he had every night. They sat cross-legged, their turbans casting shadows on their faces, and ate with the same quiet discipline. The kheer steamed in their bowls, and for the first time, they paused. One of them looked up—only for a second—and then returned to eating.

Teen Sukhia's heart raced. His mind, full of gratitude, brimmed with a question that had haunted him for months.

As they rose to leave, laying their usual wad of notes on the mat, he could not stop himself. "Maharaj… who are you?" His voice trembled. "Why me? Why bless a poor rickshaw man like this?"

The Breaking of Silence

The three men froze. The air turned heavy, colder than the winter mist outside. Slowly, the tallest among them turned his covered face toward him. When he spoke, it was in that same gruff, echoing voice that had first ordered food months ago:

"We warned you. You broke the rule."

The flame in the coal stove flickered violently, the shadows on the wall stretched long, and in the next heartbeat, the room was empty. The mat, the chowkis, the steaming bowls—all gone, as though no one had ever been there.

Teen Sukhia fell to his knees, his chest pounding. On the mat where the notes always lay, there was nothing. Only a faint dampness, like river water seeping through the floor.

And outside, through the mist, came the sound of wheels creaking—not his rickshaw's, but something heavier, older, rolling away into the night.

The Cautionary Tale of Teen Sukhia

For five long months, Teen Sukhia fed his silent visitors, and they fed his fortune. From poverty and weariness, his family rose to comfort and respect. But when he broke their only command—to never ask questions—the spell shattered.

They returned one last night, not for food, but for him. By dawn, he was gone, leaving only his abandoned rickshaw and an alarm clock frozen at 3 a.m.

In Dehradun's misty lanes, people still whisper of Teen Sukhia. On fog-heavy mornings, children swear they hear the faint creak of rickshaw wheels and the jingle of a missing bell. Some say it is only the wind. Others claim it is Teen Sukhia himself, condemned to pull a phantom rickshaw for eternity.

And so, his tale endures—a reminder that sudden fortune may come with a price and that in the silence of the night, not all visitors are of this world.

SUSHI

The first time I set eyes on little Sushi, I stared at her. She was a small beagle pup, and her grandparents and great-grandparents must have lived in this part of India, which was part of the British Raj Empire. She had no resemblance whatsoever to the local Indian Pye dog, native to the Indian subcontinent. Her rough coat with variegated brown and white, had little shades of grey, much like life. Her charming twinkling eyes had a lot to tell, and if only I understood her language, I'm sure I would be in for a big shock.

Sushi was loved by the grouchy canteen manager. His love for her was the extras of non-vegetarian food, the student's unfinished titbits. She was very special. One late evening, as the campus lay wrapped in quiet darkness, Sushi's ears perked up, and her stance stiffened. An escaped ruffian, shrouded in shadows, crept toward the gates, his intent dark and deliberate. Before he could step inside, Sushi let out a low growl that echoed through the stillness. Her sixth sense, sharp as ever, detected danger where no one else could. She darted forward, barking furiously, her sharp eyes never leaving the intruder.

The ruffian froze, startled by the unexpected resistance. Her barks roused the night watchman and several students nearby, who rushed to the scene. Cornered and caught, the ruffian was swiftly apprehended, his plan foiled. Sushi, triumphant, returned to her spot by the canteen. She was more than a puppy dog; she was a hero, a silent sentinel who always kept her beloved campus safe.

Sushi's reputation as the campus guardian was already legendary, but her next act only solidified her status. One quiet afternoon, while the students were immersed in their studies and the canteen buzzed with its usual hum, Sushi sensed something unusual.

Her nose twitched, and her ears perked as she trotted toward the back of the canteen. Hidden in the shadows near the storeroom, a student was stealthily slipping snacks into his bag, his eyes darting nervously. Sushi, with her innate knack for sensing mischief, positioned herself quietly behind him. As the student made his final move, Sushi sent out a sudden, sharp bite on his heel that startled him so much that he dropped the bag. The clattering noise drew the attention of the canteen manager, who rushed in to find the red-faced student caught in the pilfering act, with Sushi standing guard over the spilt loot.

The manager could not help but laugh as Sushi tried to wag her coiled tail, her expression almost smug. The student sheepishly apologised, and Sushi received an extra pack of biscuits and a mug of sweetened milk as a reward for her vigilance. Once again, Sushi proved she was not just the campus mascot—she was the ever-watchful protector of both its gates and its snacks!

The physical training instructor had a unique expression, but he loved sushi. He often let out a big guffaw and patted Sushi, who trotted off with him.

One chilly morning, the campus was abuzz with the usual hustle and bustle. The terrier pup trotted along her usual route, sniffing out her next treat and getting petted and loved by all the students. Little did she know, a calculated plan was being hatched by Raj Chandhok, a student known for his mean pranks and devious thoughts, along with another hallmate. They decided it would be fun to send Sushi on a long, unexpected adventure.

Pockets full of Sushi's favourite treats, Raj lured the unsuspecting pup towards the nearby train station, her tail wagging and nose twitching in anticipation. As they reached the platform, Raj's friend watched quietly, snickering with anticipation at the play of events.

The Calcutta-Howrah train was ready to depart, and Raj, with a final treat in hand, led Sushi into an empty compartment. Munching on her treat, Sushi looked up just in time to see Raj jump off the platform. He just walked off into the crowd, hoping the terrier pup would get lost in Calcutta. Sushi was not to be fooled. Confused but not alarmed, she settled into her mobile temporary new home, the train to Calcutta, eyes twinkling as she looked around.

Sushi, the beloved pup of this sprawling university campus, was missing for the last few hours. The canteen manager, who had a special bond with the little pup, was the first to raise the alarm. Students spread the word, and soon, the entire campus was in a state of worry and confusion.

As the train chugged along, Sushi made herself comfortable, charming passengers with her playful antics. Little did she know, her unexpected journey was only just beginning. Meanwhile, back at the campus, a rescue plan was being hatched. The students, determined to bring the little pup back, pooled their resources and contacted friends and family in Calcutta, hoping to track down their little furry friend before she got too far.

Sushi's adventure on the train continued, filled with new sights, sounds, smells, and friendly faces. But deep down, she missed the familiar comforts of the campus, the canteen manager's special treats, and the endless supply of students' love and attention. And so, the little terrier's journey would soon become not just a tale of adventure but also a quest to find her way back home.

Raj Chandhok, the notorious prankster of the campus, was a solitary figure in many ways. With no siblings to share his childhood and never having experienced the unconditional love of a pet, he often found himself envying the bonds others shared with their furry friends. His envy manifested in his mischievous, inhuman behaviour, targeting those who seemed to have what he lacked.

While Sushi received endless affection and attention, Raj could not help but feel pangs of jealousy. He had never known the joy of a loyal companion or the warmth of a pet's love. His pranks, often harmless and humorous, sometimes took on a meaner edge, driven by his deep-seated resentment. Raj's trick on Sushi was not just a random act of mischief but a reflection of his loneliness and desire to disrupt the happiness he saw in others.

As he watched her departure from the train platform, a fleeting moment of guilt crossed Raj's mind. But his envious nature quickly suppressed it, masking his longing for the kind of companionship and joy that Sushi effortlessly received. Little did he realise, this act would spark a journey not just for Sushi, but perhaps for Raj himself, as he confronted the emptiness in his own heart.

Sushi was not to be fooled. She smelt around the unfamiliar city and looked at all the people with soft brown eyes brimming with questions. That night Sushi slept hungry under the fruit seller's cart. Dawn brought the fruit seller back, who shooed her away and practically kicked her from under his cart.

Hungry, lost and lonely, Sushi slowly walked down a narrow lane without a clue where it would take her. Deep into the lane she found a dilapidated old house with the front gate hanging on just one hinge. Blackened with soot, age and neglect, the once lovely bungalow looked like it could collapse any minute.

The garden had wonderful fruit trees and plants overflowing with pink, buttercup yellow and red hibiscus flowers. Overladen chikoo, guava and papaya trees, along with other sweet-smelling flowering plants, added to the perfumed aura. IT WAS Heaven. “WAIT”!!

She heard chuckles of laughter, and a ripe papaya was aimed straight at her.

Sushi’s extremities froze, the hair on her back rose, her nose twitched, and she could sense and see a soft misty golden human shadow aura that moved. Not one or two, maybe five or six. They were all cheerfully playing a game ...and some more sitting on the tree branches. She jumped back almost onto the narrow lane. Her tiny body quivered, round eyes darting around, searching for safety.

A soft whimper escaped from her tiny mouth, a sound so fragile it tugged at the heartstrings. The pup’s breathing quickened, shallow and rapid, as its nose twitched, trying to make sense of the unfamiliar danger.

Realisation dawned! Those were not like the rest of the folks or young students she had met. A human ghost! They were all human ghosts having a great game of fun and mirth.

A soft, compassionate, glowing aura emanated from them; suddenly Sushi was no longer afraid. This aura was both calming and ethereal, signalling their lingering connection to the world of the living and their desire to comfort, protect, or complete unfinished acts of kindness. Now if it meant sharing a home with cheerful or sullen ghosts ...so be it!

Sushi was wide-eyed and thrilled that afternoon when she saw her otherworldly friends had shared their afternoon meal with her. They were deft, skilled at pilferage, and each had a unique claim to fame in their mortal past lives. They were close friends, as was evident in this wonderful afterlife as well.

After a week spent with them, Sushi had shared all her anecdotes and life story with her spirit friends. Her ethereal guides were astute, helping the living heal or grow before they themselves found peace. They decided to help her back to the university campus. After dinner, a motley group and Sushi made the surreptitious journey to the Howrah station at the dead of night. The train usually departed early morning, so she would have to stay hidden only for a short while. As she boarded the same train with the help of loving friends, the pup promised to come back again. They in turn promised they would visit her and her sprawling world at the university campus.

As the train pulled into the station, she smelt the familiar campus. What did she smell? Your guess is as good as mine. And then Sushi walked back all of 3 kilometres to reach her home, the canteen and the student blocks. A lot of us were very surprised and thrilled to learn that Sushi had returned home. She got hugs, love, treats and biscuits from the Pan Wala at the end of the road in front of the dormitory.

Sushi looked back just once at the road she had walked on, and her eyes twinkled. On the tree branches were three of her new friends. She saw the moving surreal golden misty auras … recognised her friend the judge and his best friends. They loved this pup and had taken the journey to ensure her safe return.

Sushi had realised her newfound friends were not restless spirits but rather guardians and protectors. They signalled their lingering connection to the world of the living and their desire to comfort, protect, or complete unfinished acts of kindness. They were helping the living while tied to their own unfinished stories.

Sushi let out a soft, gentle bark, and as her tail refused to move much, she wagged her entire body, while her tree-bound friends waved out to her!!.

This university campus was her home. Her otherworldly friends in Calcutta were deeply empathetic souls with a knack for understanding without words, seeing into the hidden layers of people's hearts. Sushi's eyes brimming with love said it all. She had adopted them forever.

The end….

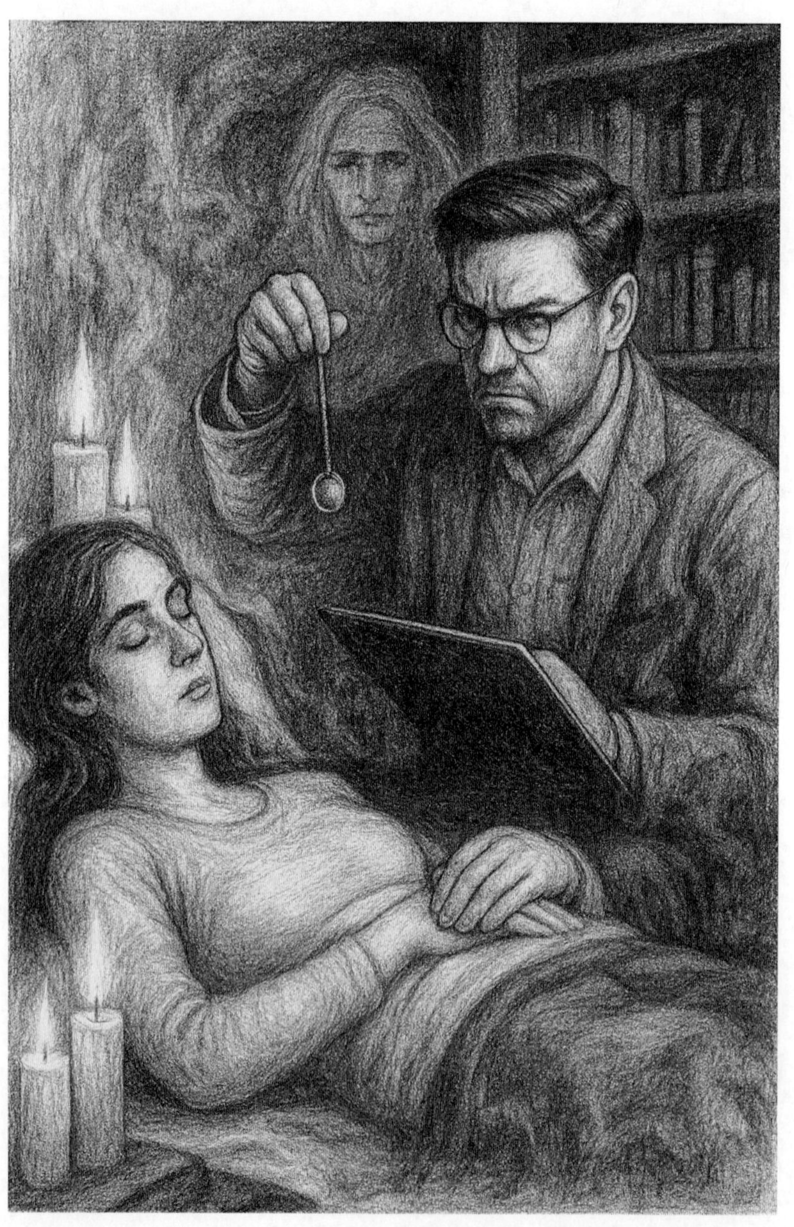

WHY ME?

The hypnotherapist's voice guides her back. The woman is in a state of deep relaxation and describes what she sees. "I see... my feet. They are small, in little black shoes. I'm wearing a dress; it's white with blue ribbons. "I'm in a park," she says, her voice trembling slightly. "I hear laughter, children playing."

The scene unfolds vividly in her mind. She is a five-year-old girl, swinging happily in the park, her nanny nearby. Suddenly, the nanny's expression changes, and two unfamiliar men approach. Before she knows it, she is whisked away in a car, her cries muffled by the bustling streets. She remembers the nanny looking away, her betrayal evident.

The ride is a blur of fear and confusion. The little girl clutches her doll tightly, her heart pounding. Eventually, the car stops, and she is led up a grand, curved staircase with polished wood. At the top, a balding man in his 40s greets her. His smile is forced, his eyes cold. "Welcome, my dear," he says, ushering her into a room filled with toys, a big chalkboard, and a comfortable bed with large, airy windows.

The room, despite its splendour, feels like a gilded cage. The little girl sits on the bed, tears streaming down her face, clutching her doll. She misses her parents terribly and wonders why they haven't come for her. Days turn into weeks, and she starts to adapt to her new surroundings. The man, who she learns to call Father, tries to win her over with gifts and kind words, but she remains wary.

Each day, she stares out of the large windows, hoping to see a familiar face, but the view remains the same. Her only solace are the toys and the chalkboard, where she draws pictures of her family, hoping that somehow, they will see her messages and come to rescue her.

Mr Lincoln's house is grand, filled with servants who treat her kindly but keep their distance. She learns that the house once belonged to his late wife and that he had longed for a child to fill the void in his life. The nanny, complicit in the plan, visits occasionally, her guilt masked by a false cheerfulness.

As time passes, the little girl begins to understand her predicament. She realises that she must play along with Mr Lincoln's wishes and pretends to be happy, laughing at his jokes and thanking him for the toys. But in her heart, she harbours a deep longing for her real family and the life that was stolen from her.

At night, when the house is quiet, she whispers to her doll, recounting the happy memories of her past life. She vows to never forget her parents and dreams of the day they will come to take her home. In her dreams, she hears their voices, calling out to her, and she finds comfort in the thought that they are searching for her, just as she is waiting for them. The house, despite its grandeur, echoed with a sense of emptiness. Servants moved quietly, their faces void of any real warmth. The little girl, now settling into this new routine, felt the weight of loneliness more acutely. She missed the laughter, the hugs, and the bedtime stories of her past life.

Her new father, Mr Lincoln, while physically present, was emotionally absent. His attempts to provide for her material needs and comforts could not compensate for the lack of genuine affection and emotional connection. The little girl, who had been used to the warmth and love of her real parents, found this new life cold and unfulfilling. Mr Lincoln often sat with her during meals, his eyes distant, lost in thoughts of his own. He would ask about her day, but there was a mechanical quality to his questions, as if he were following a script. His smiles never reached his eyes, and his pats on her head felt perfunctory.

One evening, as she sat by the window, watching the stars, Mr Lincoln entered her room. He stood there for a moment, looking at her with an expression she couldn't quite decipher. "Do you like it here, dear?" he asked, his voice lacking the softness she longed for.

She nodded, forcing a smile. "Yes, it's nice," she replied, though her heart ached for her real home. Her new father sighed, as if relieved by her answer, and left the room without another word.

As days turned into months, the little girl learned to navigate this new life. She found solace in her toys and her drawings, escaping into the worlds she created on the chalkboard. She became friends with the housemaid, Elsie, who would sneak her extra treats and tell her stories of far-off lands.

Despite the coldness of her new home, the little girl never lost hope. She clung to the memories of her parents, knowing that they were out there, searching for her. Every night, she whispered a prayer, asking for their safety and for them to find her soon.

Present Day:

The woman in the therapist's office breathes deeply, her eyes still closed. The therapist gently brings her back to the present, her voice calm and reassuring. "You are safe now. You are no longer that little girl. But you have remembered, and that is the first step in healing."

The woman opens her eyes, tears streaming down her face. The fear of loss and kidnapping that had plagued her begins to make sense. With the therapist's guidance, she begins to heal from her childhood trauma.

One day, while exploring the house, she stumbled upon a locked room. Curiosity piqued, she asked Elsie about it. The maid's face turned sombre. "That was Mrs Lincoln's room," she whispered. "It's been locked since she passed away."

The little girl felt a pang of sadness for Mr Lincoln. Despite his wealth and status, he was a man broken by loss. In that moment, she understood a part of his coldness, but it didn't make her own pain any less. She resolved to keep being brave, hoping that one day, her parents would come for her and she could leave this house of shadows behind.

As she grew older, the little girl became more adept at hiding her true feelings. She played the part of a dutiful daughter, but inside, she remained the same hopeful child, waiting for the day when she would be reunited with her family.

And so, the little girl waited, her spirit unbroken, knowing that love, true and unconditional, was out there, and she would find it again.

A lost child who keeps waiting for her parents.

The little girl sat by the window, her small hands pressed against the cool glass, eyes searching the horizon. Day after day, she waited, hope flickering in her chest like a fragile flame. Every sound of footsteps made her heart race; every knock on the door sent a surge of longing through her.

But no one came.

She clutched the worn-out doll they had given her, but it wasn't the same. It wasn't her parents; the ones she knew were out there, somewhere, maybe looking for her. She believed in her heart that they would find her. She just had to wait a little longer, through every long night and every endless day, holding on to the memory of their voices, their warmth.

Each day she whispered, "They'll come for me. They have to, and she waited for 25 years...then 40 years. Seasons changed, years slipped away, and still, she sat by that window, eyes searching for a glimpse of the life she had lost, which was becoming a faint memory with the passing years.

Her heart aged, but the child within her remained, longing, yearning, and believing against all odds. Every birthday, every holiday, she'd whisper into the silence, "They'll come for me." The world moved on, but she stayed, a lost child in an adult's body, waiting for parents who had become shadows in her dreams. She was home tutored and sent to the best private school.

Her adopted father died; he passed away one cold winter night, leaving behind the vast, empty mansion that now felt even colder. The walls that once echoed with his footsteps were now filled with silence, and the grand hallways seemed endless without his presence. Life was lonely in the big house, and she was the sole inheritor of the business and the big house.

She stood alone in the large house, staring at the faded portraits and expensive furniture, feeling like a stranger in a place that had never truly been her home. Despite all the wealth, she felt more lost and alone than ever before. As the sole inheritor of his thriving business empire and the sprawling estate, she now had everything material one could wish for—but nothing of what her heart truly needed.

Each morning, she would walk through the mansion's corridors, her fingers trailing along the walls, remembering the little girl she once was, longing for the warmth of her real family. Her father's world was now hers to manage, but every decision, every paper she signed, reminded her of the life she was forced into—the life that had kept her from her true self for so many years.

And as she looked out of those large, airy windows, she still waited. The longing had never left her, even after all this time. It was as if a piece of her soul had been frozen in that moment when she was taken, and despite everything she had gained, she knew deep down that she was still just that little girl, waiting for her real parents to come and take her home.

“Hello darkness, my old friend,” she whispered into the quiet room, the shadows her only companions. It wasn’t the first time she’d felt its familiar presence wrap around her like a heavy blanket, and it wouldn’t be the last. In the silence, she found a strange comfort, a place where her secrets, fears, and longings could be laid bare without judgement.

The mansion, though grand, was just another shadow in her life, echoing the loneliness that had followed her since that fateful day. Yet, in this darkness, there was a sense of truth—an unspoken understanding that despite all the wealth and power, she was still searching, still waiting, for something that only the light of her past could bring back.

We come to the present.

Walking to work, she often passed a home nestled between two towering trees, its weathered facade whispering tales of a time she couldn’t place. Each step past its wrought-iron gate tugged at something deep within her—a feeling she couldn’t shake off, as if the house itself was reaching out to her.

Her chest tightened, the air growing heavier, filled with an ache that was both familiar and foreign. She didn’t understand why, but the sight of the chipped shutters and the overgrown garden felt like a wound reopening. The air thickening around her, heavy with a sorrow that wasn’t hers. The overgrown garden didn’t just look abandoned—it felt wounded, like something still grieving. Memories swept over her—snapshots of a life she couldn’t fully grasp. The sound of laughter, muffled cries, and a sense of deep loss so sharp it made her breath catch, all intertwined in her mind.

Then the flicker came: a sudden rush of déjà vu. Laughter that wasn't hers. Cries muffled by walls that no longer stood. A grief so sharp it stole her breath. For a heartbeat, the house seemed alive—watching, remembering, waiting. And in that silence, she wondered if it was a memory she felt… or something that had never truly left.

She paused, bewildered, her gaze locked on the front door, which seemed to hold a thousand unanswered questions. The pain in her chest was unbearable now, as if this home had once been hers in another time, another life. Yet the memories remained just out of reach, leaving her stranded in the aching void between familiarity and mystery.

On one of her visits … SHE RECOUNTED a description of her mother, who had more children.

Her Next HYPNOTHERAPY Session:

Her body sank deeper into the couch, breath uneven as the hypnotherapist's voice guided her back. Suddenly her words spilt out, sharp and urgent, as though the memory had been waiting: "The house… I see it again—the iron gate, heavy, like it wants to close on me. The shutters are chipped, the garden wild, everything dripping with rain." Her voice trembled, then rose louder, almost defiant: "It feels wrong… The air is thick, and I can't breathe. There's laughter inside—but it twists into crying. I don't know why, but the sadness burns through me, as if I've lost something there, someone… and the house won't let me go."

The hypnotherapist's pen moved quickly across his notepad, eyes lingering on the patient's face. He nodded reassuringly, her tone calm but firm. "You're doing much better. We'll adjust the medicines slightly—nothing drastic, just something to ease the weight of these memories."

When the session ended, she rose from the couch feeling oddly lighter, though the sadness still clung like a shadow. Collecting her things, she stepped out of the clinic into the brightness of the afternoon. There was no time to linger—she had a lawyer's meeting in the next town.

Sliding into her car, she joined the slow tide of traffic. As the line of vehicles crawled forward, she turned her head almost absently—and froze. On the pavement lay an old woman, still as stone, encircled by five anxious onlookers. For a moment, the scene blurred; a chill ran through her chest. She blinked, the cars ahead pulling her forward, and then—almost without choosing—she drove on.

It struck her like a revelation. This was not just any old woman—it was her Ayah, the one she had trusted as a child. Memories surged, jagged and unfinished: the park, her toys scattered, her small hand slipping into the Ayah's… then the gleam of an expensive car, its doors swallowing her whole.

That day, everything she knew was stolen. The Ayah had not simply cared for her—she had delivered her to the man who claimed her as his own. A lonely widower, wealthy and grief-stricken, he had filled her life with privilege: the best schools, the finest universities, and eventually, the keys to his vast legacy and mansion.

She had grown into that life, building a reputation and a legal practice that carried her name with weight and respect. Yet the hollow ache of something unresolved had never left her.

Now, seeing the Ayah again—frail, broken, lying helpless on the street—she felt the wound of that betrayal crack open, raw as the day it happened. The truth was no longer buried.

The sight of the old woman cracked something deep within her. This was no stranger on the pavement—it was her Ayah, the very woman whose lullabies had once wrapped her in safety and whose betrayal had rewritten the course of her life.

On that fateful morning, she had trusted those familiar hands. Instead of guiding her home, they led her into the waiting car—and into another life entirely. She had been taken to the grand house of a widower who called her his daughter, raised her with privilege, and bestowed on her the education and inheritance of a dynasty.

The world saw only success: a sharp legal mind, an established practice, and a woman whose name carried weight. But the hollow ache within her was something no achievement could conceal. She had never reconciled the fracture of that day—love entangled with betrayal, belonging with loss.

And now, confronted with the Ayah's frail form, she felt everything collapse into one unbearable truth. The woman who had stolen her away had also shaped the very foundation of who she had become. Was she grateful? Or unforgiving? Both answers tore at her in equal measure.

She drove away, hands gripping the wheel, her head a chaotic blur of then and now. The years folded in on themselves—from the wide-eyed five-year-old clutching her doll in the park to the accomplished woman she was today.

In all those years, she had pictured her Ayah's face a hundred times: stern and tender, familiar yet distant, always with unanswered questions behind those dark eyes. But the face she had seen today was not the one of memory. It was a broken, half-dead frame, life all but snuffed out.

And yet the thought gnawed at her—could this dying woman hold the truth she had sought all her life? Could she point to the one place, the one memory, the one locked door that explained everything? The place she had longed to uncover but never found?

The road stretched ahead, but her mind was trapped between two worlds—one she had lived and one that still lived in her. The traffic pulled her forward, yet her mind refused to let go. Each honk, each flash of headlights ahead, only thickened the blur in her head. She could almost hear her five-year-old self calling, pulling her backward, whispering, ***"Don't leave her this time***."

Her hands trembled on the wheel. She had imagined this face a hundred times in her life, and now, when fate finally placed it before her, was she really going to drive away? What if the old woman's fading breath carried the truth she had hunted for decades? The one place she had always wanted to know, the one question that had shaped her entire being?

With a sharp breath, she swung the car into a sudden U-turn, the tyres spitting rainwater off the road. Her heart pounded as she retraced the short stretch back to the pavement.

The scene had not changed—the small crowd, the limp body, the faint glimmer of life in sunken eyes. But this time she stepped out, rain pinpricking on her face, and pushed through the circle of onlookers.

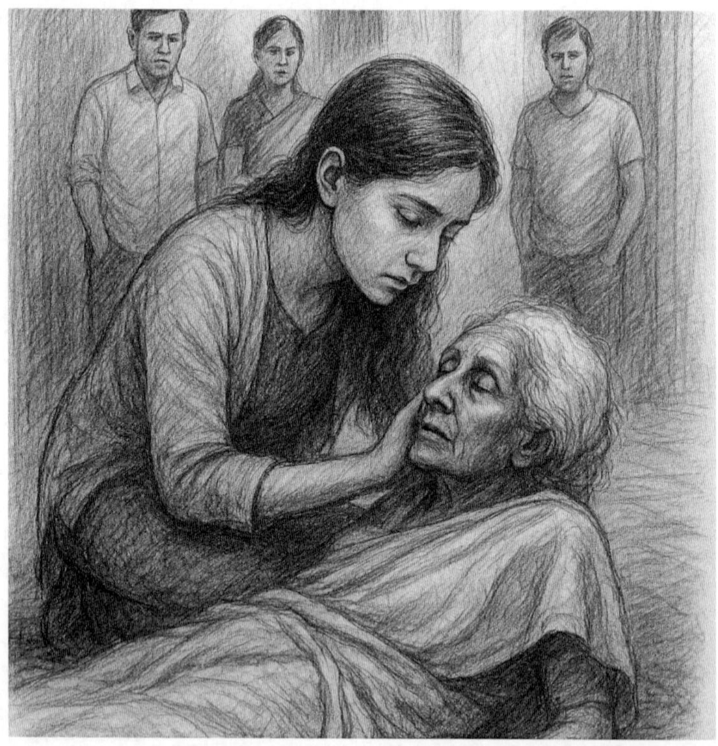

The Ayah's eyes fluttered open, cloudy but searching. For a moment, the years peeled away—she was once again the little girl with her hand in that woman's palm.

Kneeling beside her, voice breaking, she whispered:

“Show me… please. Show me what I’ve been searching for all my life.”

The Ayah’s lips moved, breath shallow, words forming slowly, as if torn between confession and silence.

The Ayah’s lips trembled, her voice rasping like wind through dry leaves. The onlookers blurred into shadows; all that existed was the dying woman and the child she had once carried away.

“The house…” she whispered, the word barely audible. Her eyes rolled for a moment, then fixed on her with sudden clarity. “The big house… the one you pass each morning. It’s where it began. Where he brought you.”

A shiver ran down her spine. The house that had haunted her every walk to work, the chipped shutters, the overgrown garden, the weight pressing at her chest—it was not imagination. It was a memory.

“Why?” She choked, her voice breaking. “Why me? Why that day?”

The Ayah coughed, each word costing her breath. “He wanted a child… someone to fill the emptiness. I thought I was giving you a better life… safety, wealth… but I stole what wasn’t mine to give.”

Tears stung her eyes. The crowd leaned closer, but for her, the world was collapsing into the faint rasp of the woman’s breath.

“There’s a room… upstairs,” the Ayah whispered, “with the blue door. The truth… is there.”

Her head sagged, the words dissolving into silence, and the faintest trace of life left her body.

She knelt frozen, her hands trembling. The house was no longer a mystery on her walk to work—it was the key to everything. And now, the dead had shown her the way back.

Present Times

That night she could not sleep. The Ayah’s words looped endlessly in her head. “The big house… the blue door… the truth is there.” The house she had passed for years, the one that unsettled her with every glance, now called to her with an urgency she could no longer resist.

By dawn, the streets were slick with rain, the air heavy with monsoon mist. She parked her car at the corner, heart pounding, and walked toward the wrought-iron gate. The place looked exactly as it always had: chipped shutters, a wild garden, and silence pressing against the walls. But now it wasn’t just a house. It was hers—and it held the secret of her life.

She pushed the gate open; it groaned like something waking from sleep. Each step up the damp stone path carried her deeper into both memory and dread. Inside, the air was stale, thick with the scent of abandonment. Dust clung to the faded wallpaper, and the floorboards creaked beneath her weight as though protesting her return.

Her eyes found it almost at once—at the top of the staircase, half-hidden by shadow: the blue door.

She stood frozen, breath shallow. Behind that door lay the answer to the questions that had haunted her since childhood. The truth the Ayah had tried to whisper with her dying breath.

Slowly, she placed her hand on the knob.

The blue door creaked open, its hinges sighing as if in relief. She stepped inside and froze.

The room was crowded with photographs—black-and-white, sepia, and faded colour prints nailed to the peeling walls. Faces stared back at her: a mother and father she barely remembered, smiling stiffly into the lens. Then more—younger sisters, brothers, and relatives whose names she could not summon but whose eyes seemed to follow her. A whole family she had been torn from, preserved here like ghosts.

Beneath the photographs lay scraps and junk, remnants of another life: brittle papers, yellowed books, and a chipped teacup. In one corner, a child's tricycle, its paint flaked but wheels still intact. Beside it, a small basket with a ragged blanket—the kind a dog might have once curled into, guarding its little mistress.

Her breath caught. The air was thick with dust, but it was more than that—it was as though time itself had been sealed in this room, waiting for her return.

Every object whispered of belonging, of roots denied. It was proof that she had not imagined the ache all these years. Proof that the house had indeed been hers long before it became a mystery.

She reached out to touch one photograph—her mother's face, serene and smiling—and the tears came, unstoppable, breaking open years of silence.

The truth had been hidden, but now it stared at her from every wall.

She wiped her eyes, but another glimmer caught her attention—a box shoved under the tricycle, its lid warped and edges yellowed with age. Kneeling, she pulled it free, the smell of mildew rising as she pried it open.

Inside, beneath brittle newspaper clippings and a child's hair ribbon, lay a leather-bound diary. Its pages were fragile, the ink faded but still legible. She turned carefully to an entry written in a steady hand:

"...the debts are mounting. I cannot feed them all. The youngest, she will have a better life if she is taken. The man has promised safety, education, and a future. It breaks my heart, but what choice do I have?

Her breath stilled. This was not theft alone—it was a bargain born of desperation.

Further pages revealed more: **a signed letter of arrangement**, confirming the widower's request for a child to raise as his own. The Ayah had been complicit, but the decision had roots in the family itself—someone had agreed to let her go.

The photographs on the wall blurred through her tears. Sisters, brothers, parents—all kept living their lives while she had been traded into another. She pressed the diary to her chest, the words cutting deeper than any wound: she had not been stolen by chance but chosen to be given away.

The room seemed to close in, the toys and scraps whispering not just of memory, but of betrayal.

She sat on the dusty floor, the diary clutched tight against her chest, her mind reeling. For years she had thought of herself as stolen, her life rewritten by strangers. But now the truth stared back at her in brittle ink: she had been chosen to be given away.

At first came the ache—a deep wound reopening. But then, beneath the grief, something else stirred: a fierce resolve. She had lived too long in shadows, piecing together fragments of memory and haunting herself with questions. Now she had the proof, the names, and the faces on the walls. Wiping her tears, she stood, her spine straightening.

These were not just ghosts—some of them might still be alive. Brothers, sisters, perhaps even cousins. They had lived their lives, carrying forward a family that had once decided her fate.

For the first time, she no longer felt powerless. She would find them. She would confront them—not just for answers, but to claim her story back.

She stepped out of the room; the blue door swinging closed behind her. It no longer felt like a mystery but a threshold. Beyond it lay a reckoning she had avoided her whole life. And she was ready.

The days that followed were a blur of determination. She pored over the diary, tracing names, cross-checking dates, and chasing down every faint clue. Old municipal records, fading birth certificates, and property registries became her battlefield. As a lawyer, she was trained to dig, to pursue threads until they yielded truth.

The reunion was not without pain. Questions burned, silences weighed heavy, and the knowledge of her "exchange" for survival still cut deep. But around the table, with photographs pulled from drawers and stories spilling into the night, she felt the ache soften. For the first time, she wasn't imagining a family. She was part of one.

She realised then that the house with the blue door had given her not just truth but a bridge back to what she had always craved: belonging.

The Search

Armed with the diary and scraps from the blue-door room, she began her search with the precision of a lawyer and the hunger of someone reclaiming her own story. Each faded photograph became a clue; each scrawled name in the margins, a trail to follow. She scoured birth registries, old land records, electoral rolls, and even obituaries. Nights blurred into dawns, her desk littered with notes, maps, and highlighted files.

Every lead felt fragile, but persistence kept her going. Slowly, a pattern emerged—a sister who was a teacher in a small school, a brother who kept a modest business in a nearby town, and cousins who had drifted far but not vanished. It was as if the scattered pieces of her lost family were waiting to be re-stitched.

The Discovery

The first knock was the hardest. When the door opened to a pair of eyes startlingly like her own, the years collapsed in an instant. Her sister—face lined by time but unmistakable—stood frozen, recognition dawning slowly. Tears came before words.

One by one, doors opened. A brother, greyer but alive, welcomed her with hesitation that melted into an embrace. Cousins filled in stories she had never heard—weddings she never attended, funerals she never mourned, lives that had carried on without her. Each meeting was a mix of joy and ache, reunion and reckoning.

Slowly, the fog lifted. One by one, fragments of her lost family emerged. Another sister—now a schoolteacher in a small town. A brother—greying but alive, running a modest shop. Cousins scattered across cities, each carrying echoes of the bloodline she had once been severed from.

When she finally stood on the threshold of her eldest sister's home, her heart pounded harder than in any courtroom battle. The door opened to a pair of eyes—older, tired, yet unmistakably familiar. In that instant, years of absence collapsed. They didn't speak at first. They simply looked, and something long broken began to mend.

The Outcome

For the first time in decades, she was no longer only a successful lawyer defined by a borrowed legacy—she was a daughter, a sister, and part of a bloodline she thought she had lost forever. The betrayal of the past could not be erased, but with each embrace, each shared memory, the wound softened.

Her search had given her more than truth. It had given her belonging. And as she stood surrounded by the faces she had once only imagined on the walls of the old house, she knew she had finally found the missing part of herself.

TIGER CALLING ......

It was the day of the great solar eclipse of the year.

Deshpande, the seasoned forest officer, had read about it in the local papers. The celestial shadow was expected to pass over around noon, and the light of day would not fully return until after 5 o'clock.

From the veranda of his cottage—a modest dwelling tucked within the buffer zone of the reserve—he looked out at the strange stillness that had settled over the jungle. The house sat in its own small clearing, enclosed by a barbed-wire fence, where the forest had been cut back years earlier. Beyond the fence stretched the deeper, wilder Tadoba forest: sal, teak, and bamboo rising like sentinels, their silence pierced only by the distant cry of a langur.

The eclipse seemed to have hushed the forest into anticipation. The birds were quieter than usual. The air was heavy, as though the jungle itself was holding its breath. Deshpande had spent years patrolling these lands, listening to alarm calls, tracking pugmarks, and guarding against poachers. Yet today, as darkness approached at noon, there was a charge in the air he had never felt before — as though the tigers themselves knew something was about to unfold.

The Cottage at Night

Deshpande's cottage had solid stone walls, one heavy teak door, and a barbed-wire boundary which made sure the jungle stopped at the fence. The bathroom and kitchen were inside, a blessing during monsoon nights when venturing out meant wading through snakes and scorpions.

The three officers — Deshpande and his two colleagues — rotated their weekly home visits. That week, only two remained in the cottage, with one colleague away visiting his family. This left the house quieter than usual, its silence amplified by the surrounding forest. At night the cottage was secure, with the only main door and gate locked, their kitchen and bathroom being inside. Every night, they double-checked the locks on the main gate and the heavy door, tested the radio sets, and kept their walkie-talkies recalibrated to forest headquarters. Beside the radio sat a small rack of licensed firearms — both rifles for anti-poaching patrols and a tranquillizer gun, should they be forced into an encounter with one of the reserve's great cats. Deshpande had always preferred the tranquillisers, though he knew well enough that a cornered tiger left little room for choices, and they did have the licence to keep firearms to guard against poaching and self-defence, along with tranquilliser darts if needed for tiger or sloth bear attacks.

Inside, the air smelt faintly of kerosene from the lanterns. Beyond the windows, the jungle stretched dark and endless, the cries of peacocks and the occasional bark of a chital punctuating the night. On that eclipse day, however, something about the silence felt different — heavier. The jungle had hushed, as though the animals themselves were waiting for something.

The Eclipse Afternoon

By noon, the sky had begun to dim. Not like the monsoon clouds he knew so well, but a strange pallor — as if the world were wrapped in smoke. Birds, confused, grew restless. Peacocks fluttered into the trees too early, chitals clustered nervously, and even the langurs sat unusually still, their alarm calls muted into uneasy chatter.

Deshpande stepped out into the cottage garden, binoculars slung around his neck, while his colleague monitored the radio. The solar eclipse had begun. Shadows sharpened, strange and distorted, falling at odd angles. The barbed wire fence gleamed with a silver edge, each thorn glinting like a blade.

The forest seemed to hold its breath. No cicadas droned. No parakeets screamed overhead. Even the constant rustle of bamboo leaves died away. It was the kind of silence that made the skin prickle — as if the jungle were watching itself in a mirror and did not like what it saw.

For the next hour, the light thinned to an eerie twilight, as though night had stolen a march on day. Deshpande watched a herd of deer gather near the lake, hesitant to drink. A lone sambar let out a deep bark — once, twice — before falling quiet again. Somewhere far off, a tiger's low chuff echoed, but it was strange, stretched, and almost mournful.

By four, the darkness had reached its deepest. The reserve looked otherworldly, as if the jungle had slipped into a forgotten age. The birds were roosting, the jackals stirring, and yet the sun was still high above — veiled by the moon's shadow.

And then, slowly, the light began to return. A single koel called. A breeze stirred the neem tree by the cottage. The animals, confused but relieved, began to scatter back into their rhythms. But the memory of the eclipse hung heavy. It had left behind a silence that did not feel entirely natural, like a pause in a story not yet finished.

Deshpande noted it in his logbook as a phenomenon of nature, but deep inside he knew the jungle had shown him something more—a reminder that here, man only borrowed time.

The Rogue Tigress

As the light returned, the forest seemed to settle — yet not fully. A koel called, the neem leaves rustled, and deer drifted back to graze. But underneath, Deshpande felt a vibration, an unease. The jungle was not done.

Around dusk, when the reserve always grew restless, a sound rose from the far end of the buffer zone. At first it was just the distant alarm call of a langur, short and clipped. Then another, higher pitched. Soon the chitals barked, sharp and insistent, their heads all turned to the same patch of bamboo.

Deshpande froze, walkie-talkie in hand. His colleague stepped onto the veranda. Together they listened. Then came the sound that silenced everything else: the dragging shuffle of a heavy body through grass.

Out of the shadows, she emerged. The rogue tigress. She limped — her left hind paw twisted, perhaps from an old snare wound. Each step was laboured, but her shoulders still rolled with raw power. Her ribs showed faintly beneath the orange and black, hunger sharpening her already haunted eyes. She paused at the edge of the clearing, nostrils flaring, ears pricked.

The barbed wire seemed laughably thin against her presence. She paced, circling slowly, her limp making her movements uneven, unnerving. Every few steps she let out a low growl — not a roar, but a grinding rumble, like stone dragged over stone.

The officers dared not move. The tigress's amber eyes glowed in the dim light, fixing on the cottage as if she knew they were there. Deshpande's finger twitched near the tranquillizer gun, but he held back. He knew her kind of hunger. One wrong move, and she might charge.

The walkie-talkie crackled suddenly with a voice from headquarters, the static slicing the silence. The tigress froze, head snapping toward the sound. Her eyes locked with Deshpande's through the gloom, then she melted back into the trees, swallowed by dark shadows, leaving only silence behind.

But it was not relief that filled Deshpande. It was dread. Because in the half-light of the eclipse and after, he had seen something more than an animal. In her limp, her hunger, and her hollow stare, the tigress carried the eclipse itself — a living shadow that had not quite left the jungle.

The Morning Patrol

By 8 a.m., the jungle was washed in the cool mist of monsoon. The downpour of the previous night had left the tracks sodden, parts of the downhill trail nothing more than sludge. The official jeeps couldn't pass — the clay had turned treacherous, with patches behaving like quicksand. Road repairs would take weeks, and tourist safaris were still a month away from reopening.

Deshpande stayed behind at the cottage, making notes, while his colleague ventured out with a walkie-talkie, a tranquiliser gun, and two daily-wage labourers to check the breached section of the road. Their task was simple: mark the worst patches for repair crews, then return before the heat thickened.

The forest was wide awake — barbets calling, peacocks screeching, and langurs bickering in the mist-heavy trees. But beneath the chorus lay a strange tension. Even the labourers, villagers from nearby hamlets, muttered nervously. They knew the signs.

The Tigress Strikes

Without warning, the langurs fell silent. A chital barked once, then again, sharper. The labourers froze, eyes darting. The officer raised his hand, scanning the bamboo thicket.

And then she came.

The limping tigress, ribs heaving, hunger sharpening every muscle, burst from the undergrowth with a guttural snarl. Before the men could react, she pounced on the nearest labourer. The sound was sickening — a neck snapped clean in her jaws, the body collapsing like a rag doll.

The second labourer screamed and bolted uphill. The officer swung his tranquiliser gun, but the tigress was already on him. She struck with one massive paw, claws raking his shoulder, knocking him to the ground. He felt her teeth closing on his arm as she began to drag him into the undergrowth, her limp slowing but not weakening her fury.

The walkie-talkie crackled wildly, his panicked voice breaking through static: "…Tiger… road… help—" before the sound was drowned in a roar.

The Eerie Pause

Back at the cottage, Deshpande froze as the garbled transmission cut out. The radio hissed, then silence. Beyond the garden fence, the jungle had gone unnaturally still — the kind of stillness that only comes when death walks the trail.

For the first time in years, Deshpande felt the boundary between forest officer and hunted man collapse. The tigress, broken and starving, was no longer just an animal. She was something else — a force that had risen with the eclipse and now claimed her due.

The Rescue

The garbled cry on the walkie-talkie jolted Deshpande into action. Within minutes, he and two armed guards set off downhill, rifles slung, mud sucking at their boots. The mist clung low to the bamboo, muffling sound. They followed the broken trail — trampled grass, a shoe half-buried in clay, and the metallic tang of blood hanging in the air.

Up ahead, they heard it: a guttural snarl, the sound of flesh dragged against wet earth. The guards raised their rifles, nerves strung tight. And then they saw her.

The tigress crouched over Deshpande's colleague, her paw pressing him into the mud, teeth locked onto his arm. Blood streaked the clay like paint. The man was half-conscious, groaning weakly as she tugged him toward the thicket.

"Fire!" Deshpande hissed.

A shot cracked, echoing through the valley. The tigress snarled, whipping around, eyes blazing. She released the officer but didn't retreat — instead, she limped forward, shoulders rolling, fury radiating from her body. The second guard fired, the bullet thudding into a tree trunk.

For a terrible instant, Deshpande thought she would charge. Her growl rumbled through the mist, chest deep and shuddering. Then, as suddenly as she had appeared, she turned and melted back into the bamboo, dragging the carcass of the first labourer with her. The undergrowth swallowed her whole.

The Aftermath

They rushed to the wounded officer, his arm mangled but still attached. He was alive, barely, eyes wide with shock. The surviving labourer, pale as the mist, emerged from the trees, trembling. Together, they carried the injured man back toward the cottage, every step heavy with the knowledge of how close death had come.

But when Deshpande glanced back, he saw it — a trail of drag marks leading into the thicket, crimson staining the clay. The jungle was silent again, as if it had already accepted the offering.

The Report at Chandrapur

When Deshpande reached Mul Road, Chandrapur, he filed his report with the Field Director and the Chief Conservator of Forests. His account of the limping rogue tigress — her attack on labourers, her hunger, her uncanny appearance — sent a ripple of unease through the room. It wasn't only the loss of life; it was the uncertainty of where she had come from.

The officials cross-checked the latest tiger census data. Tadoba's buffer and core zones were mapped meticulously: pugmarks, scat samples, camera traps, and individual ID charts of stripes. Not a single entry matched a lame tigress.

Corridor Puzzles

The administrative staff considered a possibility: had she wandered in from Pench? After all, the Tadoba-Andhari reserve was not an island. It was part of a greater chain — the Pench–Kanha–Tadoba corridor, a living belt of forest threading across Central India. This corridor was vital: it allowed tigers to migrate, interbreed, and maintain the genetic health of the species.

If the tigress had limped her way through this corridor, she should have been recorded. Camera traps across Pench, Kanha, and Tadoba logged dozens of tigers and leopards. But the limping tigress? She wasn't there.

A Vanishing Shadow

Months turned to years. Rangers laid more cameras, charted more pugmarks, and studied every leopard and tiger in the buffer and core. Reports came of healthy cubs, of male disputes, of tigresses hunting by lakesides. But never again of the limping tigress.

She had appeared in the wake of the eclipse, killed, vanished into the bamboo, and dissolved into silence. For forest officials, it remained a frustrating gap in the data. For the labourers and villagers, it became a whispered story:

A tigress born of shadow, not census. A ghost of the corridor, walking where no record could follow.

Even Deshpande, an officer of reason, felt the weight of her mystery. In his private journal, Deshpande wrote : “The eclipse did not leave with the light. It stayed, walking the jungle on four paws.”

“Science tells me she was flesh and blood. But the jungle tells me otherwise. For how can something that never entered the tally leave so deep a scar?”

THE SCEPTIC AND THE SAND

I trace my roots back to the 15th generation of Gaur Brahmins, once settled in Bengal. During the Islamic conquests, the Pancha Gauda Brahmins scattered across the north, drifting like leaves torn from their branches into Punjab, Bihar, and Odisha—and one branch westward, to Pali, near Jodhpur.

It was in Pali that the Brahmins took a new name — Paliwals. They built homes, prayed in temples, and lived in the shadow of the thriving merchant community, whose wealth and generosity made Pali a jewel of Rajasthan.

The Paliwal merchants—Jain traders famed for their riches—had businesses that thrived, magnificent havelis and temples of marble and sandstone, and generations of wealth. I belonged to this community. As an engineer, I remained an atheist, a sceptic, a man of reason — an oil engineer in Jaisalmer, trained to believe in machines, not myths.

For me, ghosts were tales for children, and jinn's were inventions for the fearful.

The Tanot posting …

My posting in Tanot, on the India–Pakistan border, was supposed to be nothing more than hard work and desert discipline. I had moved from Pali and travelled to stay with my eldest sister in an old house five kilometres from Tanot. The beautiful haveli, more than a century old, was shaded by a sprawling neem tree at the courtyard's edge.

Every morning before I left for duty, my sister—deeply devout—tied a red holy thread around my wrist, woven with tiny herbs and amulets meant to ward off evil spirits. I smiled at her fuss, brushing it aside as superstition. As a man of science, an atheist, my faith rested on my machines and training. The desert, however, had its own logic, and Tanot its own stories, even for the hardest of sceptics.

One morning, leaving at 5 a.m. for work, I kick started the motorbike and set off towards the Land Rig site. The desert air was damp with a winter chill; stars were still faintly scattered above the horizon. As I sped down the empty track toward the outpost, my headlamp carved narrow tunnels of light through the dark. Then—I saw a figure standing by the neem trees ahead.

The motorbike sputtered and came to an abrupt stop. Sweat was running down my back despite the cold, and my eyes were fixed on the motionless figure. I kept trying to start the bike, at last the engine roared back to life—and the road ahead was empty. No footprints in the sand. Just the endless desert silence.

I told myself it was a trick of exhaustion, a mirage. That night, I recounted the morning's events to my sister while having hot cups of masala tea after dinner. My god-fearing sister quietly tied a fresh red thread on my wrist, her eyes saying more than words ever could. She never tried to convert me. Tying her auspicious red threads and tending to the neem tree , she started recounting … while I sat with her, listening in silence. An atheist, still, yes — but one who knew that the desert held truths no engineer could measure.

Echoes of a Township Gone By

That khejri grove ,where the moustachioed goatherd appeared was once the heart of a small township. Traders, goat herds, mechanics with grease-stained hands, and tiny workshops hummed with life. The clang of metal, the bleating of goats, and the chatter of children once filled the lanes.

But the desert has a long memory. Shifting sands, extreme climate, and the drying up of every water source forced families to abandon their homes. Some migrated across the border in search of livelihood; others moved to Jodhpur, Bikaner, or further afield.

Those who remained – like the moustachioed goatherd, the weary mechanic, and above all, the indomitable Daadi Sa – clung stubbornly to their land, eking out survival from meagre resources.

Daadi Sa and the Neem Tree

Daadi Sa, nearly blind in her old age, refused to leave her 300-year-old haveli. Every day, she watered the small neem tree outside, humming the same lullaby she once sang to her grandson, her little Banna, who she believed would return from Jodhpur.

Her prayers seemed to breathe life into the tree. It grew faster than anyone expected, its branches wide enough to shade five people at once. Strangely, its leaves were not bitter like ordinary neem. Instead, they carried a faint sweetness— "mitha neem", the villagers said, not kadwa. People came from nearby hamlets to pluck a few leaves, believing in their healing and spiritual power, attributing it to Daadi Sa's blessings.

Her Peaceful Passing

In the cool of one winter night, Daadi Sa lay by the open courtyard, listening to the rustle of her neem tree. She whispered her grandson's name one last time, and with the lullaby on her lips, her spirit gently slipped away. When villagers found her the next morning, her face was serene, a faint smile lingering as though she had finally reunited with her family in dreams.

Legacy of the Neem and the Haveli.

After her passing, the old haveli did not crumble into ruin. Neighbours, out of respect, tended to it. They kept the neem watered, swept the courtyard, and lit a lamp on her threshold during festivals. To them, Daadi Sa had become a guardian spirit — her energy rooted in that extraordinary neem tree.

Travellers resting beneath its shade often remarked on the strange comfort they felt, as though someone invisible watched over them. The villagers would nod knowingly, whispering:

"Daadi Sa never left. She is here, in the leaves of this neem, sweet like her love."

The Ghostly Watchers

Long after Daadi Sa's peaceful passing, her neem tree became the living soul of the abandoned haveli. By day, villagers gathered beneath its shade, plucking the strangely sweet leaves and speaking of her blessings.

The Fire That Wouldn't Die

Long after the township emptied, villagers noticed a faint glow in the haveli courtyard on moonless nights. By night, the courtyard told a different story. Travellers crossing the desert at dusk sometimes whispered of a turbaned goatherd with his two silent goats standing by the neem, their eyes glowing faintly in the moonlight. Some swore they saw the moustachioed goatherd crouched by the fire, his two goats watching silently, their eyes burning like coals. By morning, only cold ash remained — but the air smelt of wool and smoke.

The Mechanic's Echo

Others claimed to hear the faint clang of iron tools, as though the old mechanic was still mending bicycles and engines in his invisible shop. Children dared each other to stand near the old shed. When the wind was still, they heard the clink of spanners and the squeal of a bicycle chain, though no hand touched them. Occasionally, a rusted wheel spun slowly, though the air was dead calm. They whispered that the mechanic still toiled, mending journeys that would never resume.

The Haveli That Never Emptied

During a fierce sandstorm, a family took shelter in the haveli. As lightning flickered, they glimpsed three figures in turbans and shawls sitting around a fire in the courtyard — the goatherd, the mechanic, and an old woman in white. The storm raged all night, yet the family remained untouched, as though shielded. By morning, the fire was gone, the courtyard bare. The villagers later said, "Daadi Sa lent you her guardians. That is why you lived."

Neighbours, who continued to maintain the haveli, swore that its rooms were never truly empty. In the still hours, they heard soft footsteps in the corridor or Daadi Sa's lullaby drifting with the desert wind. Some even believed the neem leaves carried her voice.

Children, both frightened and fascinated, told each other tales that the ghostly shepherd, the mechanic, and Daadi Sa herself had become guardians of the old home. No harm could befall anyone resting in its courtyard, so long as they respected the neem tree and the memory it sheltered.

The Final Belief

Over time, the haveli became a place of both comfort and unease. By day, it was a shelter; by night, a shrine of whispers. The villagers said the neem's sweet leaves held the essence of Daadi Sa's prayers

— and that her spirit had drawn the others back, even the restless ones, like the shepherd and the mechanic, to sit once more under her shade.

So, it was believed that the haveli never died, because its people never truly left. They lingered as guardians, shadows of a township swallowed by sand — watching, waiting, forever tied to the land they once called home.

The Eerie Moral

The haveli became legend — a place of both shelter and fear. By day, its neem gave shade and healing. By night, it was home to shadows that outlasted their bodies. The villagers said the haveli was never truly abandoned because those who had loved it never left. And on the night of her first death anniversary, several villagers saw her—sitting under the neem, rocking gently, crooning to a child who wasn't there. When they approached, she was gone, but the neem's leaves trembled as though her song still lingered in their veins.

And so, the desert taught its truth:

What people abandon, the land remembers.

Not with monuments, but with fires that reignite, wheels that turn, lullabies caught in trees, and shadows that walk the sand. The haveli and its guardians taught a chilling truth: when people vanish, their land remembers them. Not in monuments or records, but in fires that refuse to die, wheels that spin without riders, lullabies trapped in trees, and shadows that outlast the body.

The desert buries water, but not memory. And what you leave behind may one day return — not to haunt in malice, but to remind in silence. In Rajasthan, where the sands bury water but not memory, even a rational man must sometimes bow his head to whispers of the past. You don't have to believe in ghosts to feel them. But slowly, I stopped mocking her. I did not admit belief, but neither did I dismiss it. In time, he understood what his sister had always known:

Ghosts are not always to be believed, but they are always to be remembered.

For in Rajasthan, where sand buries water but not memory, stories themselves become spirits. They guard, they guide, and they linger — whether one accepts them or not.

THE WHISPERING LIBRARY IN THE HOUSE OF ST BARNABAS

Born of Soho Square's 17th-century vision, the house was raised between 1744 and 1747—its walls first silent, then steeped in wealth drawn from distant Jamaican plantations and the trade in human lives. Like many English estates of the 1700s, its grandeur was quietly built on the backs of the enslaved.

Over 280 turbulent years, the house has shifted identities—elite residence, wartime ruin, sanctuary for the forgotten. It was struck during the Blitz, restored by the Air Training Corps, and later became a training centre, a women's hostel, and finally, in 2006, a members' club with a conscience.

Since 1862, under the name "House of Charity" (and from 1951, the House of St Barnabas), it has offered shelter and dignity to those who've known homelessness—its long corridors echoing with footsteps from both privilege and pain. The House stands at the edge of history and hope, its stones holding stories whispered only to those who listen. **Now it lives on as a private members' club, where the footsteps of the elite and the humble still echo through its storied halls."**

"I was a stranger, and ye took me in."

Etched into the fireplace of the House of St Barnabas, these words, "I was a stranger and ye took me in," whisper its shadowed history. Since 1862, this enigmatic sanctuary had offered refuge to the homeless and forgotten. In 1951, the House of Charity shed its former name and became known as the "House of St Barnabas", as if it were adopting a new identity to reflect the secrets held within its timeworn walls. Even now, the air hums with the echo of lives once sheltered here—some saved, some lost, all drawn to its quiet, haunting grace. The House stands at the edge of history and hope, its stones holding stories whispered only to those who listen.

The Stranger in the Library

The fire crackled low in the grand hearth of **Barnabas House**, its embers casting fleeting shadows on the words inscribed above:

"I was a stranger, and ye took me in."

Few knew the story behind those words, but the library's hidden alcove still bore silent witness to the night a desperate man found refuge within its walls.

He arrived in the dead of winter, his clothes **soaked through with rain**, his breath ragged with exhaustion. The old steward, a man of quiet kindness, found him near the back entrance—half-frozen, clutching **a cloth bag of silver** against his chest. His hands trembled, not from the cold alone, but from the weight of what that silver meant: **his freedom, his future, his last chance to escape.**

Though his skin was lighter than most of his kin, his features carried the blend of two worlds—high cheekbones, a straight nose, and full lips that hinted at stories unspoken. His eyes, amber in the light, held something watchful and alert to the spaces where he belonged and those where he never would. The way he carried himself betrayed his lineage, one who had fled the plantations of the Caribbean, disguising himself as an English merchant. He spoke the language well enough and had practised the accent, but fear clung to his every word. **He was a man who could not afford to be seen.**

For two nights, he remained hidden in the alcove of the library, concealed behind towering bookshelves and velvet drapes. The steward brought him bread and a woollen cloak and whispered updates of the outside world. His heart pounded at every creak of the floorboards, every distant murmur beyond the walls. But here, in this forgotten corner of the house, he was safe.

On the third dawn, the steward led him to the docks, where a ship bound for **Africa** awaited. The bag of silver—once a price upon his life—became the currency of his escape. As the ship disappeared beyond the morning mist, the steward returned to St Barnabas House, **etching the words above the fireplace,** *"I was a stranger, and ye took me in,"* **as a quiet testament to the night a stranger had knocked… and had not been turned away.**

And though centuries passed, on cold winter nights, some claimed they could hear faint footsteps in the library—the restless echo of a man who once sought refuge, with nothing but wet clothes and a silver-fuelled dream of freedom.

Now St Barnabas House lives on as a private members' club, where the footsteps of the elite and the humble still echo through its storied halls."

Our true story … July 2015.

It was a chilly evening, the kind that seems to seep into the walls and linger. My son and I sat at the large oak table, the dim light of a single desk lamp casting elongated shadows across the room. Between us lay a collection of technical charts, pages worn and slightly yellowed with age.

We were deep into silver analysis—tracking trends, decoding anomalies. One stood out: a sudden bearish plunge, the result of a "fat finger" trade by a global speculator. It sent ripples through the market, hinting at a rebound.

The plan was simple: three hours of work, a quick debrief, and we'd be done. But certain pages resisted—returning to our hands again and again. The charts began to pulse, almost breathing. Patterns shimmered with a strange familiarity, and a quiet sense grew between us: the charts appearing more alive with each glance, their lines and patterns almost pulsing.

Then came the whispering. Soft at first—scattered and barely there—we assumed it was just the murmur of voices drifting up from the lower floor. The kind of thing old buildings carry in their bones. But as time passed, the sound grew clearer. It wasn't frightening, just… insistent. Like someone trying gently, patiently, to be heard. Not a chill, but a tug—on memory, on instinct, on something older than either of us could name.

I caught my son glancing over his shoulder.

"Do you hear that?" he asked softly, as if afraid to disturb something unseen.

I nodded. The sounds weren't just whispers now—they felt like thoughts brushing against ours, unspoken yet oddly familiar. Not words exactly, but impressions: urgency, longing, maybe even warning.

The room had shifted. Not in temperature or light, but in presence. As if something—or someone—had joined us, quietly observing, leaning in. One of the charts slid off the table on its own, landing face up, its lines suddenly clearer, almost purposeful.

My son didn't move.

"Did you—"

I shook my head; my eyes fixed on the chart.

It wasn't fear we felt. It was knowing. The kind that doesn't come from logic but from somewhere deeper—somewhere just beyond the veil. The whispers rose into an unintelligible chorus—no longer distant, but all around us. We left the charts behind that night, scattered on the table as we hurried out. But they didn't stay scattered.

When we returned the next day, the room was still. The charts were stacked neatly on a shelf—except one. The current year's chart lay open on the empty table, untouched yet freshly inked.

My son paused, then turned it over, a quiet thrill in his breath.

It had been waiting.

The reverse side revealed a sprawling history of silver—three centuries of crashes, peaks, and recoveries, etched in script so fine it seemed impossible. Under the artificial light, the ink shimmered faintly, like breath on glass. This was no ordinary chart. It pulsed with stories—of wars, wealth, ruin, and rebirth. A map not just of markets, but of humanity itself.

And then we saw them—markings that didn't belong. Archaic symbols, scattered like breadcrumbs between the data. The notations seemed to resonate with meaning that was just out of reach. At the very bottom, barely visible, was a line scrawled in delicate, fading ink:

"The Whispering Library"

My heart pounded. A warmth spread across my face—not fear, but something older, like recognition.

And then, faintly, the whispers returned. But they were different now.

They spoke with voices I didn't know I remembered—soft, sorrowful, persistent. Not demanding but asking. Not frightening, but near. Names lost to time. Stories buried in ledgers. Hands that once held silver are now reaching through paper and ink, longing not for revenge… but remembrance.

The dead had not returned to haunt us. They had returned to be heard.

The Whispering Library is a place where charts come to life and the past refuses to stay silent. These charts held more than three centuries of restless emotions, stolen whispers, and unspoken truths. The walls pulsed with the echoes of those who had lived, loved, and lost—trapped between pages that bled with their forgotten sorrows. By electric light, the silver ink glittered, as if the past itself longed to speak… or to escape."

I nodded, unable to tear my eyes away from the chart. The weight of those 300 years pressed against us, an inescapable finality. Silver was not merely a commodity; it was a witness, carrying the imprints of every hand that had ever grasped it. The whispers were its voice, and the truth it carried was undeniable. For thousands of years, silver has been a symbol of wealth and power—minted into coins, exchanged for lives, and fought over in war. It built empires, funded expeditions, and left a trail of exploitation in its wake. Its weight carried the burden of suffering and human lives. Beneath its shine lay a long shadow.

A shiver ran down my spine. The whispers from the night before returned—faint, steady, and now perfectly in sync with the beat of my heart. Was this a warning? A ledger not of trades, but of fates. My son looked at me, his face pale. "We shouldn't have touched it," he whispered.

A gentle hush settled over the library, as if centuries of stories had finally found their voice—and peace. The whispers faded. The air felt lighter, the room calmer. No longer a place of restless echoes, it had become a sanctuary where the past could quietly rest.

And yet, something lingered. For those who entered with open hearts, a quiet presence remained, as though the stories were not gone, only waiting.

We left the chart where it was, untouched. When I returned later, it had vanished.

But in the weeks that followed, silver's price began to rise—slowly, steadily, as if nudged by an unseen hand. It climbed toward the heights once etched on that solitary, unyielding chart.

The storm of stories had passed. What remained was a stillness filled with knowing. Silver and its existence in the future of mankind will be more than just a relic of the past—it will remain a silent force shaping technology, medicine, and industry. No longer just a currency of empires or a symbol of wealth, silver will drive advancements in renewable energy, space exploration, and medical innovation. As the world moves toward sustainability, its unmatched conductivity, antimicrobial properties, and versatility will make it indispensable. Nevertheless, like history has shown, its true value will not just lie in its shine but in the power, it holds to transform the world once again."

That was my story of "The Whispering Library"—where charts do come alive and the past refuses to stay silent. Some say the library chooses its reader. And once chosen, you're never quite alone again.

HIJLI JAIL: HAUNTING ...

It was the winter of 1970; the engineering campus was wrapped in fog and silence. Arjun, Sameer, and Ravi cycled toward the department building, its shadow falling just short of the Hijli Detention Camp — the prison that had once held freedom fighters and whose walls still seemed to breathe unease.

They locked themselves inside, the iron gate's screech echoing and destroying the night's silence. The boys settled down at their drafting tables and the steady scratch of graphite pencils reclaimed the silence.

Near midnight, Arjun rose to stretch, his thoughts drifting to the girl he once loved. But as he gazed out through the misted window, his heart jolted. Shadows shifted along the boundary wall of the old detention camp. Three figures — indistinct and barefoot—sat in silence. One raised a hand as though in salute, or warning, before dissolving into the fog.

"Did you hear that?" Sameer whispered, staring at the trembling iron gate, though no one had touched it.

Ravi muttered, "This place has memories it won't let go."

That night, their drawings remained unfinished. But in Arjun's mind, one question lingered louder than the cold: were they the only three students in the building, or had the Detention Camp lent them unseen company? He looked up from his drawing, eyes drifting to the iron-barred window. And froze. A woman's face — pale, luminous, framed by black waves of hair — stared back at him. Her beauty was haunting, her stillness unnatural. It was the second floor, the dead of night. Impossible. Yet she was there.

He forced himself back to the drafting board, but her dark eyes clung to his mind. Then came a sound: soft, deliberate shuffling, like flip-flops climbing the stairs. All three boys stiffened. "Did you lock the gate?" Ravi whispered. Sameer nodded, though doubt flickered in his face.

They crept to the stairwell. Empty. The silence was heavier than the sound had been. Then Arjun's gaze fell to the frosted glass of the main door — a faint handprint forming on the outside, though the gate was locked. A gust swept the hall; he felt warm breath at his neck, scented with mahua flowers. Childhood comfort twisted into terror.

"There… a woman," he stammered, pointing to the window. Ravi and Sameer rushed over, but nothing stirred except their own breath on the glass. "You've been working too hard," Sameer muttered, uneasily. But when the shuffling began again, closer this time, none of them spoke.

The Woman at Hijli

Next evening Arjun saw her once again at the iron-barred window — a face pale and luminous, framed by black hair, eyes dark with sorrow. Yet her gaze pinned him, pleading, ancient. Then came the breath at his neck, the sweet, heavy scent of mahua blossoms — once comforting, now terrifying. The handprint on the frosted glass, the shuffling on the stairs, the figure at the far end of the hall — all the boys fled, but the scent clung to Arjun, seeping into his clothes and his bones.

Later, he learnt the truth, whispered in fragments: she was Santhal. A child of the forests, her people had lived with rivers and earth until the Raj's hunger for land and taxes drove them to revolt. With axes, arrows, and fire in their hearts, they rose — and for this, many were caged in Hijli. She was one of them. Her youth ended not in freedom but in captivity, her spirit bound to those cold walls.

And now, she returned in shadows, in breath, in the lingering perfume of mahua — not forgotten, not at peace, her sorrow woven into the folklore of the campus.

They said she had no name. But her story lived on, carried in the chill of the corridors, in footsteps that never hurry, in eyes that appear only when the night is dead.

The Ghost of Hijli

Ask the old men at the tea stalls near IIT Kharagpur, and they'll tell you: Hijli is not only history—it is haunted.

They speak of a Santhali girl, taken with her people when the British Raj crushed their uprising. Proud and defiant, she was locked away in the Hijli Detention Camp, never to see her forests again. They say her spirit could not rest, bound to the iron bars that caged her.

Students claim to see her still — a pale face at second-floor windows, black hair wet and glistening, eyes so full of sorrow they pierce the soul. She carries with her the scent of mahua blossoms: sweet, intoxicating, and out of place in the cold stone halls. Some hear her footsteps on the stairwells at night, the soft slap of bare feet, never hurried but never stopping. Others wake to find faint handprints on locked doors, pressed from the outside.

No one remembers her name. But everyone knows her story. A child of the earth, caged for rebellion, left to linger as a shadow among the lecture halls of today.

And so, the locals warn, “Don’t stay too long at Hijli after dark. For when the mahua scent drifts on the night air, you are no longer alone. The girl of Hijli walks with you.”

“The Haunted Sceptic”

Dr. Vikram Sen, professor of structural engineering at Kharagpur, was the kind who demanded proof—formulas, data, and science. Ghost stories were, in his words, “leftovers from lazy minds and colonial hangovers.”

He never believed. Not in spirits, not in signs, not in the whispered tales of Hijli’s haunted past.

But that winter, when he was assigned an old storage room in the Department of Architecture to catalogue historical blueprints, the room refused to be silent.

Books rearranged themselves. Drafting pencils fell without cause. And every evening at 7:13 p.m., like clockwork, a typewriter clicked a single keystroke: “S.”.

Still, he insisted it was coincidence. Until the night he found the half-burnt file marked “Shaista – Class C Detainee”, which had been missing from official archives since 1931. Her photo—a striking woman with wavy black hair and a smile too full of grief—stared back at him from the folder.

The same face he had seen every night for the past week was reflected behind him in the window glass.

He no longer refers to it as a haunting. He calls it a disagreement between dimensions. He no longer works there.

The Haunting of Hijli — The Escape That Never Was

They say Hijli's walls are not just bricks and iron — they remember.

One tale, often whispered by the guards' descendants and old residents of Kharagpur, is of a young freedom fighter who once tried to escape. His name was lost in the records, erased perhaps by fear or by deliberate omission. But the story lingers like a scar.

It was a winter's night. The fog had rolled thick over the fields, muffling the cries of jackals and the clang of the iron gates. Inside his cell, he had prepared for weeks and months, loosening bricks with a spoon smuggled from the mess, waiting for the watchman's lantern to dip into shadow. That night, he wriggled out, bones scraped and raw, and dropped onto the frozen ground.

He ran. Past the neem trees, past the line of barracks. The air was sharp, the soil wet with dew. The old detention camp loomed behind him, its barbed wire glistening silver in the moonlight. Freedom was just beyond the paddy fields.

But then—the sound came. Not the bark of dogs, not the alarm bell, but a metallic scraping, as though chains were being dragged along the earth. He turned. Through the fog, he saw them: figures in white, faceless, drifting. Prisoners like him, but silent, their eyes hollow, their bodies broken in strange, impossible angles. They reached out with skeletal hands, not to help, but to hold him back.

He stumbled, fell, and tried to scream — but the air was sucked from his lungs. The next morning, the guards found him sprawled against the wall, his throat dark with bruises as if choked by unseen hands. His escape route was still there: the loosened bricks, the tunnel to freedom. But he had not made it.

Since then, the story goes, his ghost still runs the corridors on misty nights. Students working late claim to hear the frantic slap of bare feet on stone, followed by a desperate gasp cut short. And always, when the mist thickens over the old Hijli grounds, the metallic scrape of chains follows — a reminder that Hijli does not let go so easily.

For some spirits are not meant to fade. They remain, so history cannot be erased. They say Hijli holds more than history — it holds unfinished stories, echoing through time. And those who listen closely enough may still catch the whispers of a revolution... and a love... left behind.